She's Just Too Funny!

by Helen Strahinich

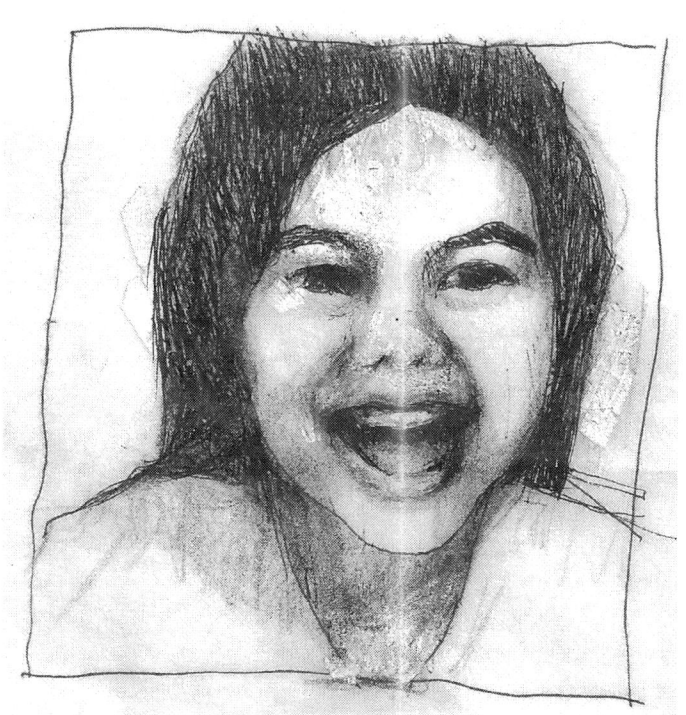

Illustrations by Lisa Kamieniecki

Copyright 2014 © Helen Strahinich

*Dedicated to my best friend, Carol Rykin,
who always makes me laugh*

Contents

One *Fossil Girl* *06*

Two *Snails* *09*

Three *Too Serious* *12*

Four *Trailside* *15*

Five *The Big Idea* *18*

Six *Joke Books* *21*

Seven *Poor Timing* *25*

Eight *The Rainbow* *29*

Nine *Packing Up* *33*

Ten *Funny Bone* *35*

Eleven *Good Timing* *37*

Twelve *Wheeling Park* *39*

Thirteen *Cool Jokes* *42*

Fourteen *Knock-Knock*	*45*
Fifteen *More Jokes*	*48*
Sixteen *Even Funnier*	*51*
Seventeen *Joke Battery*	*54*
Eighteen *Big Fat Zero*	*57*
Nineteen *Way Too Funny*	*60*
Twenty *Deep Trouble*	*63*
Twenty-One *Deep, Deep Trouble*	*66*
Twenty-Two *Sent Home*	*68*
Twenty-Three *Dead Snails*	*70*
Twenty-Four *The Milky Way*	*73*
Twenty-Five *A Bigger Idea*	*76*
Twenty-Six *Another Chapter*	*78*

One

Fossil Girl

It was lunch period. But Mel Frank hadn't even opened her cookie bag. She was too excited to eat.

The other kids at her table were laughing. They'd been telling jokes through the whole lunch period.

Mel hadn't been paying attention to their jokes. She'd been gazing at the fossil in her hand. It was a dinosaur bone. Mel's fossil was the most valuable thing she owned. It had cost every cent of her birthday money.

Mel felt proud of her dinosaur bone. In a few minutes, she would show it to her whole fifth-grade class. They'd been studying fossils all week.

Just then, Mel's lunch table cracked up. Will pounded the table with his fists. The twins, Lisa and Lou, stamped their feet. Mel's best friend, Joy, bent over laughing.

The lunch monitor rushed to their table. "That's enough," she said. "Quiet down."

Mel looked up. What was going on?

"My stomach's killing me," Lou gasped. "That was hilarious."

"Hilarious," Lisa echoed.

"I said, that's enough," the lunch lady repeated.

The laughter died down. The lunch lady stepped away.

"What was so funny?" Mel asked Joy.

By then, the lunch table was quiet. Everybody heard Mel's question.

"You missed Brandon's joke," Joy said, shaking her head.

"That's because Mel's been looking at her dinosaur bone the whole lunch period," Lisa said.

"That's because Mel is the Fossil Girl," Brandan Hamm said.

Mel scowled. But everybody else laughed.

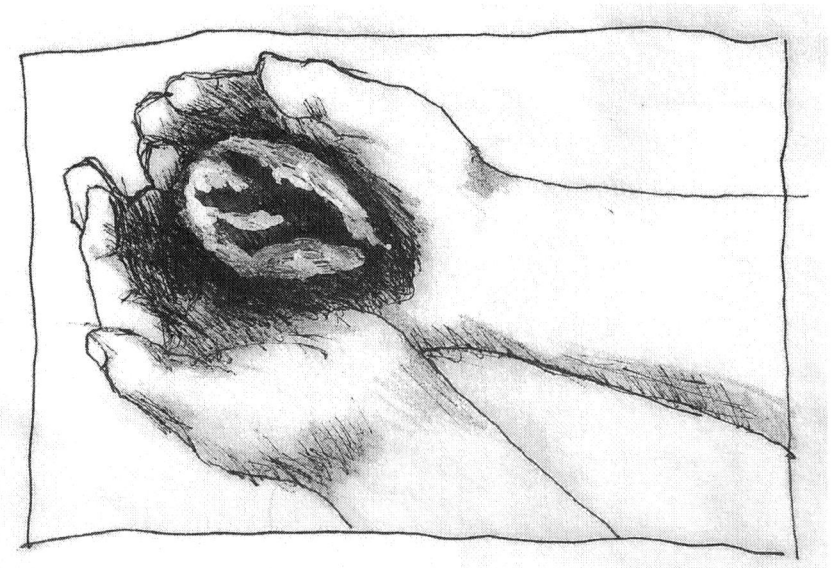

"What do you call a dinosaur that never takes a bath?" Brendan asked.

"A Stink-o-Saurus!"

Everybody cracked up.

Mel didn't get why the other kids laughed so hard. Brendan's joke was pretty lame.

And then the bell rang. Lunch period was over.

Mel felt relieved. Brandan Hamm couldn't tell another joke to make her look stupid. The thought of science class also made Mel feel better.

And then she noticed Joy walking ahead of her.

Usually Joy and Mel left the lunch room together. Now Joy was walking beside Lisa. They were talking and laughing. They were acting like best friends.

Two

Snails

The last bell rang for the end of the school day. Mel's fifth-grade class cheered. Today was Friday, and next week was April vacation. Even Mrs. Browning clapped.

Mel wrapped her fossil in paper towels. She put it into her backpack. Then she looked for Joy. But Joy had already left the classroom.

Mel wanted to remind Joy about Nature Day tomorrow. They were supposed to go to Trailside Farm together. Trailside was having a program on habitats. She hoped Joy hadn't forgotten.

Mel slipped on her raincoat and walked outside. She thought she saw Joy's red slicker in the distance. She wasn't sure. If that was Joy, she was walking with some other girls.

The rain had just stopped. The weather was still drippy. Mel walked along Dale Road, kicking puddles with her new boots. Then she turned onto Fair Avenue. Her house was just a couple blocks up the street.

Mel stopped at the brick wall that ran along the edge of her neighbor's front lawn. It was covered with snails. Snails came to the wall in wet weather. It had been raining on and off all week. Their holes must have filled with water.

Mel decided to take some snails home. She had an empty aquarium that Turtle had outgrown.

How could she carry the snails? Mel thought of her thermos. She could put them in the thermos cup.

Mel unscrewed the cup. She pulled some grass and lined the cup with the grass. Then she carefully picked three snails off the wall. She placed them in the cup.

The cup had room for one more snail. She found another big, healthy snail. She put it in.

When Mel reached her front door, she saw her mom. Her mother was collecting the mail.

"What're you carrying in that cup, Mel?" She peeked over Mel's shoulder. "Yuck!"

"I like snails," Mel said.

"Where will you put them?"

"In Turtle's old tank," Mel said.

Mel's mom nodded okay. She knew how much Mel loved animals. "Find out how to take care of snails," her mom said. "Check it out on the Internet, or go to the pet store. I don't want a bunch of dead snails in the house."

"Don't worry, Mom. You know I always take care of my pets."

Again, her mother nodded okay.

"Can Joy spend the night? Please? We're both going to Trailside in the morning."

"Sure. But you have to take Johnny with you."

Mel's younger brother Johnny was in second grade, three years behind Mel. "Do we have to? Johnny's such a pain."

"You have to," her mom said. "He's signed up for Nature Day, too."

Mel scowled. "Okay."

"I'm making hamburgers tonight. Joy's welcome to come for dinner, too."

"Can I call her on my cell phone?" Mel asked.

"Sure. Go ahead."

Three

Too Serious

Mel placed her aquarium on her desk. It now contained rocks, grass, leaves, and four beautiful snails. Mel couldn't wait to show her aquarium to Joy.

Mel took out her cell phone. This phone was for calling her parents. Or answering their calls. Mel was not supposed to call friends or to text them.

Mel tapped out Joy's number. She knew it by heart.

Joy answered on the first ring.

"Hi, it's Mel."

"Oh. Hi." Joy seemed surprised to hear from Mel. But not *happy* surprised.

"You want to sleep over?" Mel blurted. "Then we can go to Trailside in the morning. Mom says you can come for dinner, too."

Joy didn't answer.

Mel felt her stomach sink. "Can you come?" she asked again.

Still, Joy didn't answer for a while. "I can't," she said, finally. Then Joy got quiet again.

Mel's throat tightened. "You want my mom to pick you up in the morning on our way to Trailside?"

"I can't go," Joy said.

"Why not?" Mel asked. "We made plans."

"I forgot," Joy said.

"You forgot?"

"Yeah, and I got invited to a slumber party," Joy admitted.

Mel remembered how Joy had walked out of the lunchroom with Lisa. She wondered whether Joy was going to a party at Lisa's house.

"I wish I got invited," Mel said.

Joy sighed. Then she gave Mel some advice: "You're too serious. All you think about is fossils and animals. Other kids like to have fun. They like to laugh and tell jokes. You should try to be more fun. Why do you think Brandon Hamm is so popular?"

Mel didn't answer. Everybody knew that Brandon Hamm was the Funniest Kid in fifth grade. Mel wanted to tell Joy that she liked to have fun, too. But she couldn't get out another word.

The phone was quiet for several minutes.

"Well, I got to go," Joy said.

Four

Trailside

"I'm not going to Trailside," Mel told her mother the next morning.

"I know you're disappointed about Joy," her mother said. "But I paid for Nature Day. You're going."

Mel didn't speak during the ride to Trailside. "Take the camp bus home after the program," her mother said. "I'll have a nice lunch waiting for you."

When Mel entered the Nature Center with Johnny, an instructor named Danika greeted her.

"Hey Mel," she said, grinning. "You're in my group today."

"Oh," Mel answered.

"We're gonna have a blast," Danika said.

Mel shrugged.

Danika gave her a concerned look. She started to ask Mel if she was okay. But Mel turned away.

A few minutes later, Danika gathered her group. Mel was sure the other kids in the group were all younger. Kids her age were out having fun with their friends. They weren't spending their Saturdays with little kids at the Nature Center.

Danika interrupted Mel's gloomy thoughts. "This morning we're studying three habitats: pond, plain, and pine forest. We've got a lot of work to do, so let's get going."

As they hiked toward Parson's pond, Mel straggled behind. Most days, she'd be keeping up with Danika. She'd drink in every word that came from the mouth of the pretty red-headed instructor.

But today Mel was feeling sorry for herself. Her best friend Joy had abandoned her. She was the oldest kid here. And her mother didn't understand her. Nobody did.

When they reached Parson's Pond, Mel stood at the back of the group. Danika pointed out different water reeds and told them about the turtles and ducks. Mel didn't listen. She dug in the sand with her shoe.

"Who knows what that is?" Danika asked pointing to a large gray bird perched on long, thin legs.

"Is it a gull?" a boy asked.

"No, it's not a gull," Danika said. "Does anybody else have an idea?" She glanced at Mel who hadn't even heard her question and wasn't looking up.

"It's a great blue heron," Danika said.

The group gasped, as the heron snagged a wiggling frog in its long beak. Still, Mel didn't look up.

As they left the pond, Danika spoke with Mel. "Are you okay?" she asked.

Mel nodded without saying a word.

For the rest of the morning, Mel walked at the back of the group. She didn't smile. She never answered a question. Danika asked her if she was okay three times. Three times Mel nodded without saying a word.

Five

The Big Idea

The Trailside bus let Mel and Johnny off in front of the library. It was just a few blocks from their house.

Mel took three steps. And then she stopped. She had a Big Idea.

Mrs. Browning often asked her fifth graders to find the Big Idea in their reading. A Big Idea was the most important point. Everything stuck together around the Big Idea. Everything made sense.

Mel had been trying to figure out what to do about Joy and the other kids. Nothing had made any sense. And now it did. Thanks to her Big Idea.

"Come here, Johnny," she called to her brother.

Mel had stopped in front of the library. Johnny was now several steps ahead of her.

"I want to pick up some books," she explained.

"But we don't have our library cards," Johnny said.

"They know us," Mel said.

Mel and Johnny walked into the library. Mrs. Sands, a librarian, greeted them. "How are you today?"

"Fine, thank you," Mel said cheerfully. She was feeling much better now that she had her Big Idea.

Mel walked into the youth section. "Hi, Mel," said Mrs. Case, who was in charge there. "I just got a great new book on worms. Would you like to borrow it?"

"No thank you," Mel said.

Mrs. Case smiled but she looked surprised. "Don't forget to turn off your cell phone," she said.

Mel nodded and turned off her phone before walking toward the stacks.

Mel passed by the nonfiction books. She usually browsed there for nature topics, but not today. She passed the hobby section. She often stopped there, too, but not today. And then, she halted in front of a shelf that said *Joke Books and Riddles*.

Mel thought about taking every book on the shelf. But there were too many. She counted out fifteen books. Then, she made a stack and tried carrying them to the checkout desk. She didn't make it. The books fell all over the floor.

Mrs. Case came to her rescue. "Would you like a bag?" the librarian asked.

"Yes, please."

Mrs. Case opened her desk and pulled out a plastic bag for Mel. A few minutes later, Mel arrived at the front desk with fifteen joke books and two picture books for Johnny.

"Looks like you found what you were hunting for," Mrs. Sands said. "By any chance, did Mrs. Case tell you about the new worm book?"

Mel nodded.

Then Mrs. Sands checked out Mel's books. "Wow, you've got a lot of joke books," she said. "These must be for a fun school project."

Mel hesitated before she answered: *"Oh, yes!"*

Six

Joke Books

As Mel stepped into her house, her mother raced from the kitchen into the hallway.

"Oh, Melanie," she said. "Thank goodness." Then she hugged Mel.

Mel was puzzled. Her mother only called her by her real name when she was very worried or very angry.

"What's wrong?" Mel asked.

"Danika called me from Trailside," her mother explained. "She thought you were sick. I couldn't reach you on your cell phone. I almost went out looking for you."

Mel shook her head. "I'm fine," she said. "Johnny and I went to the library. Mrs. Case made me turn off my phone. Why are you always worrying?"

"It's a mother's job to worry about her children." She hugged Mel again. "Well, I'm glad you're fine,"

Then she hugged Johnny. "Both of you go wash your hands. The food's on the table. You must be starving."

Mel dropped her bag on a kitchen chair. She and Johnny washed their hands at the sink. Then they sat down for tuna sandwiches, carrot sticks, and pickles.

"So how was Nature day?" Mom asked Johnny.

"Great!" he said. "We dug up worms and found tadpoles at the pond. We saw deer tracks and a raccoon. It was fun."

"I'm so glad," Mom said.

"What about your program, Mel?"

"Boring," Mel said.

"So what did you bring home in the bag?"

"Books," Mel said.

"I got books, too," Johnny said. "We didn't even need our card at the library."

"They know you both, because you're such good readers," Mom said.

After lunch, Mel helped her mother clear the table. Then she ran upstairs for a pad of paper before running back down to the kitchen.

"Do you have a pencil, Mom?" Mel asked.

"Right here," her mother said, pulling a pencil from a blue jar by the sink.

Mel sat down at the kitchen table and took out her pile of joke books. She opened the first one and started reading.

At the end of the first page, she copied her favorite joke. Then she turned to her mother.

"Hey, Mom, what did the boy tornado say to the girl tornado?"

Her mother looked up from the sink. "I don't know. What did he say, Mel?"

"Let's take a spin."

Her mother smiled. "Very cute," she said. "Who told you the joke?"

"I took out some joke books from the library."

"I didn't know you were so interested in jokes."

"I thought it would be a good idea," Mel said. "I wanted

something to do over spring vacation. I don't have any plans. No plans at all."

"You could have Joy over."

"She's busy."

"What about Courtney? You haven't seen her for a while"

"Maybe," Mel said.

"What about Laurie?"

"Maybe," Mel said.

"You always have a good time with Courtney and Laurie."

"Maybe," Mel said.

Then she went back to her joke book.

Mel was sure this vacation was going to be boring. But at least she had her Big Idea. Maybe jokes weren't as interesting as worms. But they made sense with her Big Idea: She was going to get funny this vacation. Not just a little funny, but really, really funny. Funnier than Brandon Hamm.

"You know where hams come from?" she said to herself.

"OINK!"

The joke made her laugh. She was sure it would work on the other kids, too.

Seven

Poor Timing

"Dinner," Mel's mother called from the hallway.

"Just a minute," Mel shouted from her bedroom.

"Right now," her mother called back. "Dad's home and food is on the table. Now."

Mel wanted to practice her new jokes one more time. She had read a whole joke book after nature camp and copied down her favorites. She had just spent the last half hour memorizing four jokes. But she wasn't quite ready to try them out on her family.

"Come on, I mean it," her mother called. "The food's getting cold."

"I'm coming!"

A minute later, Mel entered the dining room. Her mother was already serving the spaghetti and meatballs.

"Yummy," Johnny said. "Give me more."

"Eat what's on your plate first," Mother said.

Then everybody was quiet. They were all enjoying the food.

"Delicious, Honey," Dad said. "I think your sauce is better than my mother's."

Mom grinned. "But you'll never tell her."

"Of course not," he said.

Everybody laughed.

Their laughter reminded Mel of her Big Idea. She decided to try out a joke. "What do you call a turtle that flies?" Mel asked.

"Did you learn about turtles at nature camp?" her mother asked.

"It's a joke, Mom," Mel said, scowling. "Real turtles don't fly."

Dad and Mom both laughed at Mom's silly question.

"So what do you call a turtle that flies?" her mother asked.

"A shellicoper."

Mom and Dad smiled.

"Very cute," Mom said.

"I don't get it," Johnny said.

"Shellicopter: A turtle has a shell," Dad explained. "And a helicopter flies, so a shellicoper is a flying shell or flying turtle."

"Now I get it," Johnny said.

Mel was upset. Nobody had really laughed at her joke. And Dad had to explain it to Johnny.

Maybe it wasn't a good joke, after all. Mel decided to try again. "What happens when a duck flies upside down?" she asked.

She waited a second, then said: "It quacks up!"

Johnny howled. Mom and Dad grinned.

"I don't get it," Johnny said.

This time, Mom and Dad laughed out loud at Johnny.

Thanks a lot," Mel said. "You don't laugh at my jokes. Then you laugh like crazy over Johnny's dumb mistake."

"It's all about timing," Dad said.

"What do you mean?" Mel grumbled.

"It's not just what you say, but how you say it and when you say it."

"What do you mean?" Mel asked, frowning.

"You can't just rush through a joke," Dad explained. "You have to wait a moment before the punchline, and then. . .WAMMY! The best comedians have great timing."

"So my timing wasn't good?"

"It wasn't bad, honey," Mom said.

"And your joke was very funny," Dad said.

Mel scowled.

"I don't get it," Johnny said.

Mother and Dad tried to hold back their laughter. But it didn't work. They burst out laughing and couldn't stop.

Mel made another face. "Thanks a lot," she said.

"We're sorry, honey," Mother said.

"What's with all the jokes, anyway?" Dad asked.

"I'm practicing for school," Mel said.

After that, they were all quiet. Dad took another meatball.

"How do I get good timing?" Mel asked.

"Either you're born with it or you're not," Dad said.

Mel scowled.

"I'm sorry, honey, but I'm just being honest," Dad said. "With the right timing, you can always make people laugh. But it doesn't matter how funny the joke is, if you don't have good timing."

"Well, I don't agree," Mom said. "Practice makes perfect."

Eight

The Rainbow

When Mel woke up on Thursday morning, she went to her window. It was still drizzling. But rays of sunshine were breaking through the clouds.

Mel searched the sky for a rainbow. Rainbows were good luck. And that's exactly what she needed. Good luck.

So far, it had been the most boring vacation ever. Joy was busy. Laurie and Courtney were both out of town. To make matters worse, the rain had kept her inside all week.

Mel had worked on puzzles. She'd played games with Johnny. She'd played cards with her mother. She'd watched movies on TV.

But mostly she'd been studying her joke books. By now, she was more than half way through her pile.

Mel had tried out a few more jokes on her family. Each time, they had laughed politely. Each time, her mother had said the joke was cute. Each time, Johnny had exclaimed, "I don't get it." And each time her parents had laughed at Johnny.

Mel never got the reaction she hoped for. She wanted

her family to laugh so hard over her jokes that their stomachs hurt. The way kids did with Brandon Hamm.

Mel concluded that her timing still wasn't right. Her father had said you were born with good timing. But her mother had said practice makes perfect. Mel wondered who was right. She hoped her mother was.

At that very moment, a giant rainbow appeared in the brightening sky. It was beautiful. Mel had never seen such a big, beautiful rainbow.

There was a superstition that you could find a pot of gold at the end of a rainbow. Mel knew there was no such thing. She had read about rainbows.

Mel knew that rainbows appeared after a rainstorm. They happened when the sun was starting to come out, but when some rain was still falling. The rainfall acted like a giant prism in the sunlight. The prism broke up the sunlight into all of its colors. The result was a red-blue-green-yellow-violet rainbow.

Yes, Mel knew what made rainbows. Even so, she was sure that rainbows were good luck. So she made a wish on the rainbow overhead. *Let me be funny, really, really, really funny. Lots funnier than Brandon Hamm. Let me be so funny that I make every kid in my class laugh. So funny that I make my parents laugh. So funny that nobody can stop laughing at my jokes.*

Then Mel ran downstairs to tell everybody about the beautiful rainbow.

They hurried out the door to the front yard. The grass was still wet, but the rain had almost stopped. The enormous rainbow glowed in the sky.

"Wow!" Johnny shouted.

"I've never seen such a huge rainbow in my whole life," her mother said.

When the rainbow began to fade, they went inside for breakfast. Mel didn't have to get dressed. It was vacation. She could stay in her pajamas all morning. Her mother didn't even pester her about brushing her teeth.

Mel sat down at the kitchen table with a bowl of cereal. She was smiling. The rainbow had lifted her spirits.

"Well, I have some good news," her mother said. "We're all going to Wheeling Park tomorrow. The weather's supposed to be wonderful."

"Hooray!" Johnny shouted. "I love Wheeling Park."

Mother turned to Mel. "You should pack your bag before bedtime," she said. "We're leaving early tomorrow morning."

Nine

Packing Up

After supper, Mel went to her room to pack her bag. She was glad about the trip to Wheeling Park. It was a fun place.

Mel finished packing her clothes. She put her outfit for tomorrow on her desk chair. Then she thought of her joke books. She had finished twelve of them. She packed the last three books in her bag.

Mel looked at the pad of paper with all her favorite jokes. She counted them. There were 158 jokes. She had memorized maybe 24 jokes.

The problem was the jokes weren't organized. If she organized her list, she could pick the right kind of joke at the right time. For instance, she could easily find the "spaghetti and meatballs" joke to tell at dinner.

Mel was good at organizing. Her teacher had said so. In fact, Mel was the best in her class at putting things into categories.

A category was a group. Things which were alike fit into the same category. Animals were one category. Turtles fit into the animal category, because turtles were a kind of animal.

Food was another category. "Spaghetti and meatballs" fit into that group.

So, Mel looked over her list and made up some categories:

animal jokes
food jokes
school jokes
holiday jokes
birthday jokes
clothes jokes
plant jokes
weather jokes
history jokes
science jokes
math jokes
knock-knocks
riddles
puns

She came up with fourteen categories in all. Then she put each joke into a group. In the end, she had 15 jokes left over. She placed them in the "left-over" category.

Mel packed her joke pad at bedtime. Before she went to sleep, she thought about the rainbow and her wish to be really, really, really funny. She wondered whether her wish would come true.

Ten

Funny Bone

Saturday morning Mel woke up early. Everybody else was still asleep. Mel felt like she'd had the best sleep of her life.

She got dressed. Then she went to the bathroom to wash her face and brush her teeth. She still had to pack her toothbrush for the trip.

There was a full-length mirror on the bathroom door. Mel decided to practice some jokes in the mirror.

She stood in front of the mirror and told this joke out loud:

A girl goes to see her doctor. The girl has a candy cane poking out of her right ear. She has a pretzel sticking in her left ear. She's got a blueberry in her right nostril. She has a peanut in her left nostril.

"*What's wrong with me, Doc?*" *the girl asks.*

"*You're not eating right,*" *the doctor answers.*

Mel started laughing. The joke had hit her funny bone. She tried to hold back her giggles. Mel didn't want to wake up Mom, Dad, or Johnny. But she couldn't stop laughing.

Maybe her great night's sleep had charged her joke battery.

Then she tried another joke on herself: *Why did you invite a bunch of goats to your house for a sleepover?*

Cause they always love to kid around.

Why in the world did you invite a bunch of pigs?

Cause they always go hog wild.

Again Mel almost rolled on the floor laughing.

Wow, she was really funny today. She didn't want to stop: *What's black and white and red all over?*

A zebra that has diaper rash.

And a skunk with a sunburn.

Mel bent over with laughter. She tried to think of something sad to stop her giggles. But it didn't work.

So she decided she'd better stop joking.

Mel wondered how she'd made herself laugh so hard. Were today's jokes just extra funny? Was she in a great mood because of the trip? Was it the rainbow? Or had her joke battery done the trick?

Eleven

Good Timing

An hour later, the alarm went off in Mel's parent's room. Mel raced in. "I got to tell you this joke," she said.

"Not now, Mel," her Dad said. "Save it for later."

Mel didn't argue. She knew her parents wanted to get to Wheeling Park early.

So Mel waited patiently while everybody ate breakfast and packed the car.

Finally, they got in the car and set off for Wheeling Park. Mel was sitting in the back seat with Johnny. She could try out a joke on her family—at last.

"How do you know when an elephant is going on vacation?" Mel asked. She paused, and counted out *one, two, three,* for good timing. Then she said, "He packs his trunk."

Mel's mother cracked up. Her father guffawed. Johnny laughed. And then he said, "I don't get it."

But this time, Mel's parents ignored Johnny. They were still laughing at Mel's joke. A full minute passed before they stopped.

"That was really funny," her dad said. "It was a perfect joke for the start of our vacation."

Mel grinned. "Thanks, Dad," she said.

"And you had good timing," he added.

Now, Mel understood what he meant. Good timing was like riding a bike. At first it seemed like you'd never learn. But once you got the knack, it was easy.

Mel started telling knock-knock jokes, one after another. Each time she counted out different beats, sometimes more, sometimes fewer.

Finally, her mother said: "My stomach hurts from laughing. No more jokes for now."

"Just one more," Mel said.

"Please," Johnny said. "Let her."

"Okay, go on," her mother said.

"Knock, knock."

"Who's there?" Johnny shouted.

"Minnie."

"Minnie who?"

"Minnie more jokes to tell."

Twelve

Wheeling Park

Mel's family arrived at Wheeling Park before lunch time. Mel and Johnny raced to their cabin. It sat near the edge of a winding creek. Mom and Dad arrived a minute later with their bags.

The cabin was one big room. It had a bunk bed for Mel and Johnny. A couch pulled out into a double bed for Mom and Dad. There was a tiny kitchenette and a bathroom off the main room.

Mel climbed onto the top of the bunk bed. "This mattress feels really hot," she said.

Her dad looked up. "That's odd," he said.

"Very strange," her mother said.

Mel bounced up and down on the mattress. The springs of the bed squeaked.

"I know what's wrong," she said. "The mattress has. . ." Mel paused, counting out *one, two, three* beats. "SPRING FEVER!"

Mel's parents laughed.

"You've got a million jokes. Don't you?" her dad said.

"Just about," Mel said.

Everywhere they went, Mel told a joke. At the creek, they stopped to watch some ducks. "I'm surprised at how many different kinds of ducks are here," Mom said.

"What's another name for a duck?" Mel asked.

Mom and Dad shook their heads.

"Flyer quacker," she said.

"What do you call a bird nest?"

"Cheep housing."

At lunch, Mom served a fruit salad.

"Oh, no!" Mel shouted. "My salad's naked."

Johnny laughed. "No, it's not," he said.

"Yes, it is. My salad's completely naked. . ." *one beat, two beats, three beats. . .* "No dressing!"

In the afternoon, Mel's family took a hike. They passed through a forest. It seemed like a million squirrels had left their nests at once. The squirrels were running everywhere.

"I've never seen so many squirrels at one time," her mother said.

"They're looking for food," her dad said.

"Can we feed them?" Johnny asked.

"You're not allowed to feed the animals at the park," Dad said.

"What did a boy squirrel give to his girlfriend before he left town?" Mel asked.

"Forget me nuts."

Whenever Mel told a joke, her family laughed. She seemed to always have the right joke for the right time. And she never ran out. In fact, she told more jokes on Sunday than on Saturday.

Finally, her mom said: "You've entertained us all

weekend, Mel. It's been lots of fun. But now it's time to have a quiet ride home."

Mel didn't mind. She was kind of tired from all the joking. Her mom was right. It would be a good idea to rest now.

Besides, she wanted to charge her joke battery for school tomorrow.

Thirteen

Cool Jokes

Monday morning, Mel was putting her jacket into her school locker. Joy walked into the coat room.

"Hi, Mel," she said.

"Hi."

"I called you on Saturday, but nobody answered the phone," Joy said.

"We went to Wheeling Park," Mel explained.

"That's cool," Joy said.

"So how was your slumber party?" Mel asked.

"Nothing great," Joy said.

They were quiet for a minute.

"So how was Wheeling Park?"

Mel shrugged. Her feelings were still hurt. She didn't want a long conversation with Joy right now.

And then Mel remembered her jokes.

"I had a bad fall on Sunday," she said.

"Really?" Joy asked.

"Yeah. I was unconscious for eight hours."

"Wow that's terrible," Joy said.

"Yeah, my mom could hardly wake me up," Mel said.

"So how did it happen?" Joy asked.

"I fell asleep," Mel said. And then she started laughing.

Ben Lee and Zack Adams had been listening. They cracked up.

Finally, Joy got the joke. She started laughing, too.

"Good one," Joy said.

Mel grinned. Her jokes were working. And she was the center of attention. She decided to try another one.

Mel started jumping up and down, up and down.

"What's going on?" Joy asked. "Why are you jumping?"

"I just took some medicine," Mel said, then counted *one, two, three* beats. "And I forgot to shake the bottle."

By now, the coat room was full of kids. Most of them were laughing. A couple fifth graders were actually pounding on the walls.

And then Brandon Hamm walked in. "What's so funny?" he asked. He seemed annoyed.

"Mel just told some cool jokes," Ben said.

Brandon scowled. "Yeah, sure," he said.

"What do Brandon's family and *pigs* have in common," Mel said.

"What?" the kids shouted. "What?"

"They're all a bunch of Hamms—Yummy, yummy," Mel said.

Brandon turned bright red. He wasn't used to being the brunt of a joke. Everybody in the coat room cracked up.

"Yummy, yummy!" Zach repeated.

"Yummy, yummy!"

"Yummy, yummy!"

"Yummy, yummy!"

Just then the bell rang. Mrs. Browning came into the coat room. "Vacation's over," she said. "It's time to settle down."

Fourteen

Knock-Knock

The school day ended like it began. With Mel telling jokes.

A crowd of kids had followed Mel to the playground. "Tell another one, Mel," Joy said. "Tell another one."

"Yeah, tell another joke," Lisa begged.

"Okay," Mel said. "What's green and flies zig-zig?"

"What?"

"What?"

Mel grinned. "A drunken super-pickle."

Everybody cracked up. Ben and Zack fell to the ground. The two boys laughed loudly and kicked their feet in the air. HAhhhhhhhHAHAHAHAhhhhhhhhh!" Lisa screeched. "That's so funny. My stomach hurts from laughing."

Mel wasn't finished. She knew knock-knocks for half the kids on the playground.

"Knock, knock," she said.

"Who's there?" Lisa asked.

"Lisa."

"Lisa who?"

"Lisa you can do is share your sandwich with me."
Everybody laughed, and Mel went on.
"Knock, knock," she said.
"Who's there?" Ben asked.
"Ben."
"Ben who?" Mel shook her head.
"Ben eating garlic and onions, haven't you?"
They all laughed louder.
"Knock, knock," Mel continued.
"Who's there?" Stan Michaels asked.
"Stan."
"Stan who?"
"Stan back, cause I'm gonna barf up my lunch."
Mel went on and on, until every kid was roaring.
Finally, she said, "I better get home, or my mother's going to send out the police."
And then, a siren screamed up the street.
"Oh, no," Mel said, pretending to be upset. "The cops are coming for me."
The kids started laughing again.
"My mom's the same," Lisa said.
"Mine, too," Ben agreed.
"Well, I better go," Mel said. "See you later."
"Can I call you tonight?" Lisa asked.
"Sure," Mel said.
"Can I call you, too?" Zach asked.
"Sure," Mel said.
Mel wrote down her cell-phone number for five kids. She knew she wasn't supposed to give out her number. But

her parents wouldn't find out. Then she raced home. She was much later than usual. She hoped her mom wasn't worried.

When Mel got home, her mother was still upstairs in her office. Mel saw Johnny in the living room. He was napping in front of the TV.

"I'm home!" Mel shouted.

Her mother came to the top of the stairs. "Everything okay?" she asked. "You're late."

"Everything's great," Mel said.

"So how was school today?"

"Everybody loved my jokes."

"That's nice," her mother said. "Do you have any homework?"

"Not much," Mel said. "I'll do it later."

"Don't put it off for too long," her mother warned.

Fifteen

More Jokes

Mel felt tired when she woke up on Tuesday morning. She tried to remember how many kids had called her last night on her cell phone. But she had lost track. A million kids had sent her text messages, too. Her mom almost caught her using the cell phone.

After that Mel had practiced some new jokes. She had not even started her homework before going to bed.

Mel went into the kitchen the next morning. "Good morning," her mother greeted her. "What do you want for breakfast?"

"I'm not really hungry," Mel said.

"Well, you have to eat something. How about a bowl of cereal?"

So, Mel's mother gave her a bowl of cornflakes. Mel took a few bites. When her mother left the room for a minute, she emptied the bowl into the sink.

Before Mel reached the door, her mother asked: "So did you finish all your homework?"

"Yes," Mel lied. Then she gave her mother a look that said *I can't believe you asked me that.*

"Good girl," her mother said, smiling.

Mel's stomach sunk. She felt a little sick. She had never lied to her mother about homework before. She'd never had to. Today was the first day she had not finished her homework. Ever.

Mel didn't say a word all the way to school. She practiced her new jokes in her head.

Her mother chatted with Johnny. She stopped the car in front of the school. Mel opened the door.

"Today is sign-up for judo at the Y," her mother said. "Be sure you come home right after school. That class fills up fast. If we don't get over there right away, you won't get in."

Mel had been asking to take judo for months. "Okay, Mom," she said. "I won't forget."

As Mel walked into the school yard, half a dozen kids greeted her. "Hi, Mel," they shouted. "Hi, Mel."

"Hello, boneheads," she said.

Everybody cracked up. It wasn't the words, which were silly. It was the way Mel greeted them that made everybody laugh.

"Tell a joke," they said. "Tell a joke."

Mel stopped in the middle of the playground. "Okay, what are the three greatest things about school?"

"What?"

"What?"

"What?"

Mel smiled. "June, July, and August," she said.

Everybody howled with laughter. Mel noticed that Joy

wasn't there. She wished Joy could see her now. Joy had told her she should lighten up. And she had.

"Tell another joke," the kids begged.

"Tell another joke."

"What does the gardener say when his veggies make too much noise?"

"What?"

"What?"

"What?"

"Peas, shut up!"

The kids laughed again, louder this time.

And then the bell rang for the start of school. Mel was glad. For the first time, she was actually tired of telling jokes.

It was fun being popular. But not as much fun as Mel had imagined. Being popular took too much time and hard work. You had to think about what other kids thought of you. You had to be a certain way, the way they expected you to be.

Kids expected Mel to be funny now. So she had to be funny all the time. No matter what she had to be funny.

Sixteen

Even Funnier

A dozen kids followed Mel home again after school. She felt like the pied piper. The only difference was kids tagged after the pied piper for his music. They followed Mel for her jokes.

But Mel was running out of jokes. She'd have to learn some more tonight. Or recycle the old ones tomorrow.

Mel was relieved when she reached her house. She was tired from all the joking. She opened the front door. But her audience would not let her go.

"Tell one more joke," the kids begged. "Just one more joke."

"No can do," Mel said. "I'm already late. My momma's gonna be mad."

"Come on," they begged. "Just one more joke. You're funnier than Brandon Hamm. Much, much funnier."

Mel couldn't resist that compliment. "Okay. What's green and sings?"

She paused a moment, while everybody waited for her answer. "Elvis Parsley."

Then Mel retold a couple of jokes that she'd used on

Monday. Finally, she waved goodbye and darted into the house.

Her mother was waiting for her.

"What's going on, Mel?"

"What do you mean?"

"You're late," she said. "We're not going to be able to sign up for judo."

"I don't care."

"But you've been begging me to sign you up for weeks."

"I changed my mind."

Mel's mother shook her head. "What's gotten into you?" she asked.

Mel didn't answer. And then the cell phone rang in her pocket.

"Who's calling?" her mother asked. "That phone is only for calls between Dad or me and you."

"It must be Joy," Mel said. "I think I gave her my number. Don't worry. I'll tell her I can't talk."

Mel slipped upstairs before her mother could say another word. She had lots of homework for tonight, and she still had Monday's homework to finish. But her phone never stopped ringing

Finally, her mother came upstairs and opened that door. "Get off that phone this minute," she said.

Scowling, Mel said goodbye to her classmate.

"Now give me the phone."

Mel frowned and passed her mother the cell phone.

"And do your homework."

"I only have a little left," Mel lied.

"So finish it," her mother said.

"You're mean," Mel said. "You just don't want me to have any fun."

Mel's mother shook her head. "Just finish your homework," she repeated.

When her mother turned away, Mel picked up a new joke book. She could do her homework later.

Seventeen

Joke Battery

On Wednesday morning, Mel had trouble waking up. She had stayed up late practicing new jokes. She didn't want her joke battery to run low.

Mel took a long time coming downstairs for breakfast. Her mother told her three times to hurry up.

When Mel stepped into the kitchen, her mother felt her forehead. "Well, you're not sick," she said. "You're not even warm. What's wrong with you, Mel?"

"Nothing," Mel answered.

"I think it's this cell phone," she said, handing the phone to Mel. "You can have it in case of an emergency. But I'm taking it back after school."

Mel didn't argue. She was just happy that her mother didn't ask her about her homework. She hadn't finished it. Again.

Mel raced into the classroom after the bell rang. The other kids were already seated. Mrs. Browning was collecting their book reports. Mel hadn't even finished reading her book.

Mel went into the coatroom to put away her jacket. She

took her time. Maybe Mrs. Browning wouldn't ask for her book report.

Mrs. Browning was at the blackboard writing down some multiplication problems. Her back was to the class. Mel slipped into her seat.

When Mrs. Browning turned around, she looked at Mel. "You haven't given me your book report yet," she said.

"You won't believe what happened," Mel said.

Mrs. Browning gave her a puzzled look

"My dog ate it," Mel said.

Her classmates howled. But Mrs. Browning scowled. "You don't have a dog, Mel," she said.

"I told you that you wouldn't believe it," Mel said.

A few kids gasped. And then everybody in the classroom laughed loudly — everybody except Mrs. Browning. She frowned. "It's not a joke, Mel," she said.

"Well you won't believe what *really* happened," Mel said.

"What really happened, Mel?"

"My little brother Johnny ate my book report," she said.

This time, the kids roared. Half the class pounded their desks. The rest stamped their feet.

"Stop laughing," Mrs. Browning growled.

"We can't stop," Lisa said. She was grinning, but her eyes looked scared. "Mel's too funny. She's just too, too funny. When she tells a joke, we can't stop laughing."

"Well you'd better stop this minute," Mrs. Browning said.

After the room got quiet again, she gave Mel her sternest

look. "You can tell Johnny that I gave you a zero on your book report," she said.

"But I'll bring it in tomorrow," Mel said.

"I'm sorry, but I won't accept it tomorrow," Mrs. Browning replied.

Then she turned to the class. "Now you'd all better do those math problems on the board, or every one of you will get a zero," she said.

Mrs. Browning returned to her desk, wrote on a sheet of paper, and handed it back to Mel. All it said was "0."

That did the trick. Nobody whispered another word.

Eighteen

Big Fat Zero

At lunch time, several kids followed Mel into the cafeteria. But today there were fewer kids at her table than yesterday.

"Boy, you were really funny this morning," Ben Lee said.

"High-lair-ee-us!" Zach Adams said.

Mel felt her chest swell like a balloon filled with joy. It was fun being funny.

"Mrs. B was mean giving you a BIG FAT ZERO," Ben said, grinning.

Everybody laughed at the words "BIG FAT ZERO".

And Mel felt her pleasure balloon burst.

But then she told a joke. "Why was the strawberry so sad?" she asked.

"Why was the strawberry so sad?" the kids shouted.

"Because she was in a terrible jam," Mel said.

Everybody roared with laughter. The kids were laughing so loudly that everybody in the cafeteria stared at their table.

And then the lunch monitor walked over. "That's enough," she said.

But the kids at Mel's table couldn't stop laughing.

"I said that's enough," the monitor repeated.

"I can't stop," Ben said.

Now, Ben looked a little scared, like Lisa during Math class.

"She's too funny," Zach said, pointing at Mel and giggling some more.

"Yeah, it's her fault," Ben said, gasping for air.

"She's way too funny!" Zach repeated.

And then Mel tried one of her jokes on the lunch lady.

"I bet your mother was a weight lifter," Mel said.

"How in the world did you guess?" the monitor answered sarcastically.

"Because she raised such a dumbbell," Mel answered.

Ben and Zach cracked up. When the lunch lady shot them an angry look, the boys kept laughing. But they both looked scared.

Before the lunch monitor could say another word, the bell rang for class.

Mel and her table-mates raced from the cafeteria, still laughing loudly.

"Do you think we'll get in trouble?" Ben asked.

Mel glanced over her shoulder. The lunch lady had her hands on her hips. She was glaring at her. Mel just hoped she didn't know her name.

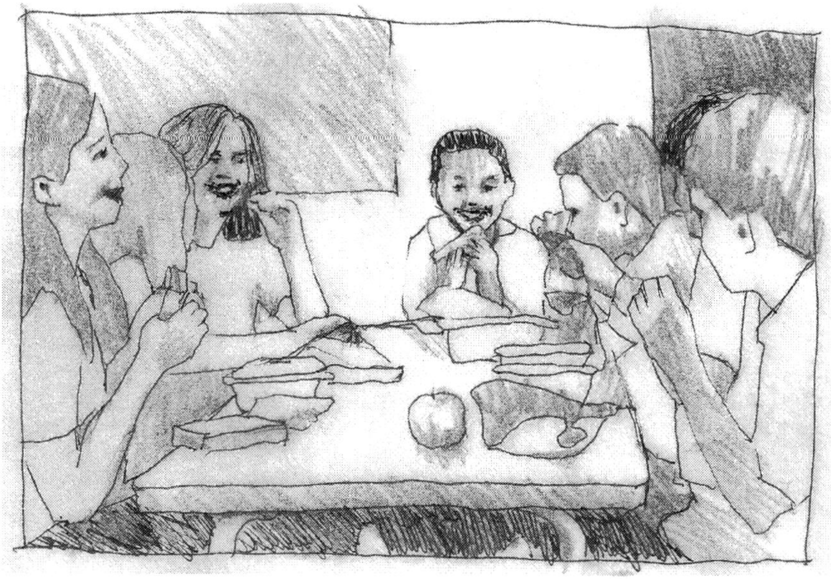

Nineteen

Way Too Funny

Wednesday night, Mel's mother forgot to take away the cell phone. But it didn't ring at all. Mel received a few text messages, but only a few. So, Mel had plenty of time to practice new jokes.

Thursday morning, Mel walked across the playground. She saw Ben and Zach. She waved and started racing toward them. The boys saw Mel, but they didn't wave back. They ran into the school building instead. Mel wondered why.

Mel was disappointed. Her humor battery was supercharged. She needed to tell some jokes right away.

Mel walked into the coatroom. Lisa and Lou were there talking with Will. Mel felt much better. Now she could try out her new jokes. But everybody left the coatroom as soon as they saw Mel.

Mel noticed the kids all looked worried. No, they looked scared. What was wrong? Mel couldn't figure it out.

Mel had trouble concentrating in math class. She took out a joke book during reading. She wanted to give the kids a joke-a-rama at lunch.

When the lunch bell rang, nobody followed her into the cafeteria. Joy was the only kid who sat at her lunch table.

"Where is everybody?" Mel asked.

Joy didn't answer.

"Where is everybody?" she shouted.

Still, Joy didn't answer her. She was concentrating on her lunch.

Mel shook Joy's arm to get her attention.

Joy put down her sandwich. She looked at Mel, and her mouth turned into a frown. Then she took earplugs out of her ears.

"Why are you wearing earplugs?" Mel asked.

"I don't want to hear any more jokes," Joy answered.

"Why not?" Mel asked.

"Because I can't stop laughing at your jokes," Joy said. "You make me laugh till my stomach hurts. I can't stop even when I try."

"I thought you liked my jokes," Mel said.

"I did at first," Joy said. "But now you're too funny. And you're getting yourself and everybody else into trouble."

"You think I'm too funny?"

"Yes, way too funny."

"How can anybody be too funny?"

"You don't know how to be serious anymore," Joy said. "When you open your mouth a joke always pops out."

"You're just a kill-*joy*," Mel said, grinning.

Joy tried not to laugh at Mel's pun on her name. But she burst out laughing. "See what I mean?" she said. "You're too funny. I can't help laughing at your jokes, no matter what."

"Knock-knock," Mel said.

But Joy didn't answer Mel. She quickly put the earplugs back in her ears. Then she took her lunch tray and left the table.

Twenty

Deep Trouble

Mel stopped in the girl's bathroom after lunch. It was empty. She stood in front of the mirror and practiced a joke. She made herself laugh so loud that her own stomach ached.

Boy, was her joke battery in over-charge. No wonder. She'd been holding in her jokes all day. Nobody seemed to want to hear them.

Maybe Joy was right. Maybe she was too funny.

The second bell rang for the start of class. Mel raced down the hallway. She slipped into the classroom.

Mrs. Browning was passing around science handouts. The other kids were already seated. Mrs. Browning looked at Mel and frowned. "You're late again," she said. "And I just heard what happened at lunch yesterday."

Mel sat down and picked up a science sheet. It was a diagram of a volcano. "Who can tell me something about volcanoes?" Mrs. Browning asked.

Mel raised her hand.

"Yes, Mel," Mrs. Browning said.

"A volcano is a mountain that's got hiccups," Mel said.

The class burst into noisy laughter. Mel thought their loud

giggling sounded like a volcano erupting. And *that* idea made her laugh.

"It's not funny, Mel," Mrs. Browning said.

But Mel felt great. The kids were laughing at her jokes again. Finally.

"Why was the mama volcano mad at the baby volcano?" Mel asked.

Nobody said a word. Nobody even moved.

So Mel answered: "Because it lost its top."

The kids roared again.

"Quiet!" Mrs. Browning said. Then she turned to Mel. "One more joke and I'm sending you to see Mr. Holland."

Suddenly, the classroom became absolutely silent. Mrs. Browning had never sent a pupil to the principal. Not all year.

What would Mel do next? Everybody was waiting to find out.

Mel didn't know what she was going to do, either. She felt thrilled and nervous at the same time. The kids were laughing at her jokes. That was exciting. But she was getting herself into deep trouble. That had her worried.

Mel's throat seemed to be full of hot air. Her ears seemed ready to pop — like a volcano.

Mel knew that she should stop telling jokes. She should say she was sorry and shut up. But she couldn't stop. "What does the mama volcano say to the papa volcano?"

A few kids gasped at Mel's rudeness. Mrs. Browning scowled.

"I lava you more than you lava me," Mel said.

Everybody cracked up again. Some kids pounded their desks. Mel was so funny.

But Mrs. Browning wasn't laughing. "Quiet!" she shouted.

The kids couldn't stop laughing.

"Okay, I've had enough."

Mrs. Browning tore a sheet of paper off a pad. She wrote a note and folded it. She walked to Mel's desk and handed her the note. "Now go to the office and give this to Mrs. Homer." Mrs. Homer was Mr. Holland's secretary.

The room got so quiet Mel could hear herself breathing.

She stood up and walked to the door. "How are a teacher and a volcano alike?" she asked.

As she stepped through the door, she shouted: "When they blow their tops, you better WATCH OUT."

Then she saluted her classmates and slammed the door.

Twenty-One

Deep, Deep Trouble

Mrs. Homer told Mel to take a seat in the front office. Mel sat down.

She looked at the clock. It was 1:00 p.m.

Every time somebody walked into the room, they stared at Mel. She wondered whether they knew that she was in trouble. She had never *ever* been sent to the principal's office before.

Ben Lee peeked into the office on his way to the boy's bathroom. "You were so funny," he whispered. "But now you're in DEEP TROUBLE." He giggled and ran off.

Ben was being mean. But he was right. Mel was in deep trouble. Deep, deep trouble.

Mel looked at the clock again. It was only 1:15. It seemed like she'd been sitting there for hours.

What if Mr. Holland forgot all about her? What if he made her sit there until the last bell at the end of the school day?

Mel imagined that last bell ringing. The hallway would fill up with kids talking and laughing. Teachers and parents and kids would crowd into the office. And Mel could slip out the door and go home with everybody else.

The thought of such a happy ending to such a terrible day made Mel smile.

Just then Mel's mother walked into the office. She glanced at Mel. But she didn't speak to her. She didn't even whisper her name. The secretary ushered her into Mr. Holland's office.

A bell rang. It was the next to last bell. Mel heard a million kids running down the hallway. They were making lots of noise. But her heart was pounding louder than their shoes.

Twenty-Two

Sent Home

A few minutes later, Mel's mother stood in front of her. "You've been sent home for the rest of the day," she said. "I'm going to get your homework from Mrs. Browning. Just wait here until I get back." Then she turned and walked out the door.

Mel looked down at the floor. She had to fight back tears. She didn't want anybody to see her crying.

It seemed to take her mother forever to get her homework. Mel tried not to think about what Mrs. Browning was telling her. She tried harder not to think about how mad her mother must be.

Mel wished she could time-travel backwards. She would take back all the jokes she had told in science class today. And the rude things she'd said to Mrs. Browning. If only she could time travel backwards.

Finally, Mel's mother returned. "Let's go," she said.

They walked together down the hallway, out the front door, and down the sidewalk to the car. Mel's mother didn't say a word all the way home.

Mel felt like she had a rock in her throat. She couldn't swallow. She could hardly breathe.

When they got inside the house, Mel's mother faced her. "I want to show you something," she said.

Mel followed her mother up the stairs and into her bedroom. Her mother went to the desk and picked up the small tank. She handed it to Mel.

"Look," she said.

Inside the tank were the snails Mel had taken home two weeks ago. She had forgotten all about them. She couldn't remember the last time she had given them water or leaves. She couldn't even remember the last time she had looked at the tank. The snails were all dead. The tank smelled.

"I don't get it, Mel," her mother said. "You used to love animals. You cared about lots of things. I always thought you were one of the most interesting kids in the world. Now it seems like everything is a joke to you."

Her mother looked at the tank. "Do you think *this* is funny?"

Mel stared at the tank again. *The poor snails,* Mel thought. *What have I done? I love animals.* Mel felt the rock in her throat loosen. Then she started to cry.

"I'm sorry, Mom," she said. "I'm really, really sorry."

Twenty-Three

Dead Snails

Mel sat down to do her homework. But she kept thinking about the tank with all those dead snails. She knew she had to clean it out.

She stepped over to the tank. It smelled worse than a dirty trash can. Or bad milk. Or an angry skunk.

Mel's throat swelled again. "This is the worst thing I've ever done," she whispered.

When Mel finished cleaning the tank, she went back to her homework. Finally, she could concentrate again.

Mel's cell phone rang. She didn't want to talk to anybody. So she left the phone in her backpack. But it kept ringing.

Mel took the phone out of her backpack and turned it off. At that moment, Mel's mother stamped into her room.

She shook a letter at Mel. "This phone bill is enormous," she said. "You must have been texting constantly these past few weeks. Even though you knew that phone was not for fun. Dad is going to hit the roof when he sees this bill. Now give me that phone."

Mel held out the phone to her mother. "Don't tell me you've been texting up here," her mother shouted.

"I turned it off," Mel said.

Her mother looked at the phone, but she was still frowning. She slipped the phone into her pants pocket and left the room.

Mel's day kept getting worse and worse. What else could go wrong?

Mel's dad got home early—probably because of her troubles at school. What had her mother told him? Was he going to give her one of his Big Lectures? What kind of punishment were they going to think up?

Mel waited for her dad to come up to her room. But he didn't come up.

She heard her mother putting plates and silverware on the table. But she stayed in her room until her mother called her for dinner. Then she slipped into the dining room and sat down.

Mel was afraid to look up. She knew everyone was staring at her.

Johnny bounced in his seat, giggling. "Mel got in trouble at school today," he announced.

"Yes, I heard about it," Dad said.

He stared at Mel and shook his head. Mel kept her eyes glued to her plate.

"I'm very disappointed in you, young lady," her father said. "Your behavior at school is totally unacceptable. And that cell phone bill." He banged the table with his fist. *"Look at me,"* he said.

Mel looked up. Her father was glaring at her. "Do you think we're rich or something?" he asked. "Your mom needs a new computer for work, and now she'll have to wait. Do you think that's fair?"

Mel shook her head no. She felt tears rising in her eyes. But she fought them back. She couldn't stand it if little Johnny called her a crybaby. He was the baby in this family, not her.

Mel waited for her dad to continue with his lecture. But he turned back to her mom and told her about his day.

Mel pushed her chicken around her plate. She loaded her French fries with ketchup. And then she pushed them around the plate. Finally, she pushed her peas under her chicken and potatoes.

"May I be excused?" she asked in a whisper. "I have lots of homework."

Her dad looked at her mom. Her mother just shrugged.

"Go ahead," he said.

Twenty-Four

The Milky Way

Mel went to her room and finished her homework. Then she finished all the assignments she'd missed this week. She even read most of the book that she was supposed to read over her last vacation.

By the time Mel stopped, she felt sleepy. She put her homework in her book bag. Then she noticed the joke books on the table by her bed. *No more joke books for me,* she thought. She was tired of being the Class Clown. She'd rather be Fossil Girl. Maybe Mrs. Case still had that book about worms. . . .

No, she didn't want to be Fossil Girl again, either. But if she wasn't the Class Clown, and she wasn't the Fossil Girl, what would she be?

Mel didn't know the answer.

Mel put on her pajamas and brushed her teeth. She went downstairs to kiss her parents goodnight.

"You know you'll be punished," her father said.

Mel nodded.

"For starters, we'll be taking away your cell phone," he said. "Before you get it back, you'll have to do extra chores to help cover our big bill."

"And you'll be grounded," her mother added.

Mel nodded again. For some reason, she didn't feel any worse after hearing about her punishment. Her troubles weren't over. But they wouldn't go on forever.

"Goodnight," her dad said.

"Goodnight, honey," her mom said.

Mel kissed her parents and went back to her room. Before she turned out her lights, she thought about the weather. She was wondering if there was going to be rain tomorrow. If there was rain, there might be a rainbow. And then she could make a new wish. She'd wish herself not to be too funny.

She looked out her window. The sky was clear. A zillion stars sparkled overhead. It looked like no chance of rain. No chance at all.

Mel decided to make a wish on her first star of the night. But she had no idea which star that might be. So she made a wish on the entire Milky Way. Maybe that would work.

Mel shut out the lights. She got under her covers and closed her eyes. For the first time in two weeks, she didn't practice any new jokes. She just fell asleep.

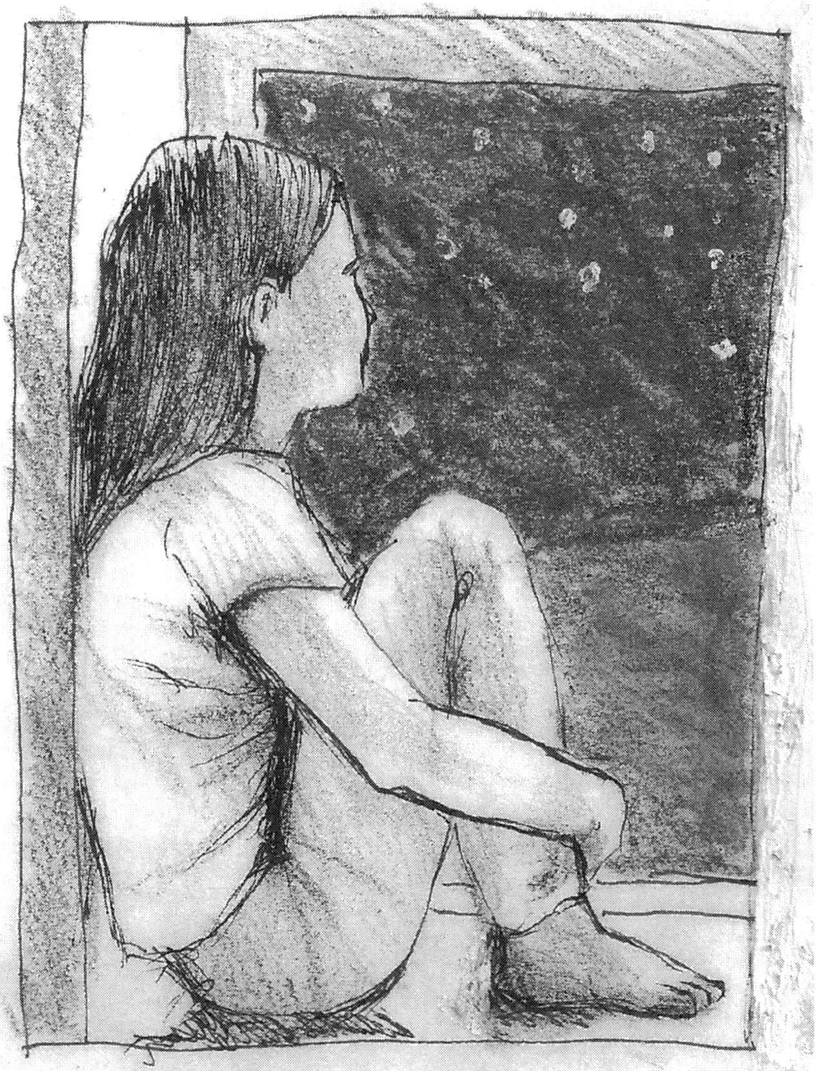

Twenty-Five

A Bigger Idea

The next morning Mel woke up before the alarm went off. She'd had the best night's sleep ever. She thought about yesterday. It was like a bad dream that was already starting to fade.

Maybe it was just a dream.

Mel turned her head and saw the joke books by her bedside. No, it wasn't just a dream.

Right before vacation, Brandon Hamm had called her Fossil Girl. And her best friend had abandoned her to spend time with the popular kids. That's when Mel got her Big Idea. That's when she decided to be really funny. So she could be popular like Brandon Hamm.

Her Big Idea had worked. She stopped being Fossil Girl and started being the Class Clown. She made all the kids laugh until they rolled on the ground. She got to be popular—too popular.

Then she got to be too funny. And everybody got into trouble—especially her. She got into Big Trouble.

This past week was not a dream. But maybe it was more

like one chapter in a book. And things could start to change in the next chapter.

The last chapter had one Big Idea. That Big Idea was about joking and being popular. Making kids laugh had been fun. Being popular had, too. But they had stopped being fun after a while.

Mel knew she needed a new Big Idea. The old Big Idea was just for one chapter. Mel needed a bigger idea for the book that was her life.

She could go to school today and be different. She could start over. She could have fun and be funny without getting into trouble. She didn't have to try so hard to be popular.

Mel had learned that being popular wasn't the most important thing in the world. She had also learned that she didn't have to be serious all the time. She could enjoy reading about worms *and* jokes.

She didn't have to be the Fossil Girl *or* the Funny Girl. She could be both things at the same time. Maybe she could even be more than two things at once. No matter how many things she was, she would still be herself.

That was it. That was the Big Idea that could work for a whole book, not just a single chapter. Mel could be herself which could mean lots of different things. And even those things could change. Her book would probably have many new chapters.

But before she went on to the next chapter, she had to finish the last one. It was not quite done.

First, she would apologize to Mrs. Browning. Then she would sit down and do school work. She would pay attention all day. She would not tell one joke.

Twenty-Six

Another Chapter

Mel got dressed. She washed her face and brushed her teeth. She went downstairs.

Her mother was fixing pancakes. That was Mel's favorite breakfast meal. She was surprised. Her mom only fixed pancakes on the weekend.

She put a big plate of pancakes in front of Mel. "I thought you might be hungry," she said. "You didn't eat much dinner last night."

"Thanks, Mom," Mel said.

Her mother sat down at the table between Mel and Johnny. A couple minutes later, her father joined them. Pancakes were everybody's favorite breakfast.

Mel finished her plate. "The pancakes were delicious, Mom," she said.

"Glad you liked them, Mel," she said, smiling. Her mom knew Mel was trying to be on her best behavior.

"You know I won't act up again," Mel told her parents. "You don't have to worry."

"We're not worried, Mel," her dad said. He smiled, too, the same knowing smile as her mother.

"And I'll always do my homework."

"We know, Mel," her mom said.

Mel hugged her mother and then her father.

"I think we've got our daughter back," her father said.

Mel's cell phone rang. It was sitting on a counter. Her mother answered it. "It's for you, Mel," she said, scowling. "Keep it short. And tell them not to call you on this phone." She passed Mel the cell phone.

Mel's stomach sunk. Some kid must want her to tell a joke. Well, she wasn't going to tell jokes today. Not even one. Maybe she'd tell a few jokes next week, but not today.

Mel picked up the phone. "Hello," she said.

"Hi, it's Joy. You want to come over tonight?"

Mel smiled. Joy still wanted to be her friend. "I don't think my parents will let me," she said. "But I'll ask." Mel turned to her mother. "Can I go to Joy's tonight?"

Her mother looked at her dad, and he shook his head no. "You're grounded."

Mel picked up the phone "I'm grounded," she said. "I'll probably be grounded until I'm 20 years old"

"Well, I'll see you at school."

"See you," Mel said.

Mel closed the phone and handed it back to her mother.

"If you settle down, maybe you can have Joy over next weekend," her father said. He looked at her mother. She nodded in agreement.

"Okay, let's get going," her mom said. "Or you're going to be late again."

"I don't want to be late," Mel said. "I've got a lot of homework to turn in."

Then she ran to get her book bag.

Acknowledgments

I started working on this book about eight years ago, and it's gone through several drafts since then. Thanks are due to two writers groups for their critiques: Becky Cheston, Dan Wilbach, Richard Edgar, and Andrea Tunarosa reviewed a final draft. Becky Cheston, Lisa Moore, and Karen Feldscher read an earlier version.

My daughters Nicki and Vanessa are my endless source of inspiration. Writing this book brought back memories of their youthful pleasure in jokes, the cornier the better.

Last but not least, I'm grateful for the help of my supportive husband John, my most trusted reader and editor.

These are some of the books that I read for inspiration while I was working on SHE'S JUST TOO FUNNY!

BEST RIDDLE BOOK EVER, by Charles Keller (Sterling, NY, 1997)

FUNNY YOU SHOULD ASK, by Marvin Terban (Clarion, NY, 1992)

IT'S RAINING CATS AND DOGS, compiled by Charles Keller (Pippin Press, NY, 1988)

KIDS' KOOKIEST KNOCK-KNOCKS, by Jacqueline Horsfall (Sterling, NY, 2006)

KING HENRY THE APE ANIMAL JOKES, compiled by Charles Keller (Pippin Press, NY, 1989)

NUTTIEST KNOCK-KNOCKS EVER, by Matt Rissinger and Philip Yates (Sterling, NY, 2008)

RIDDLES AND MORE RIDDLES, by Bennett Cerf (Random House, NY, 1960)

SILLY KNOCK-KNOCKS, by Joseph Rosenbloom (Sterling, NY, 2001

TOMFOOLERY, by Alvin Schwartz (Lippincott, NY, 1973)

YOU MUST BE JOKING!, compiled by Paul Brewer (Cricket Books, Chicago, 2003)

Made in the USA
Middletown, DE
05 April 2025